TRUCKS

WHIZZ! ZOOM! RUMBLE!

by Patricia Hubbell

Illustrated by Megan Halsey

Amazon Children's Publishing

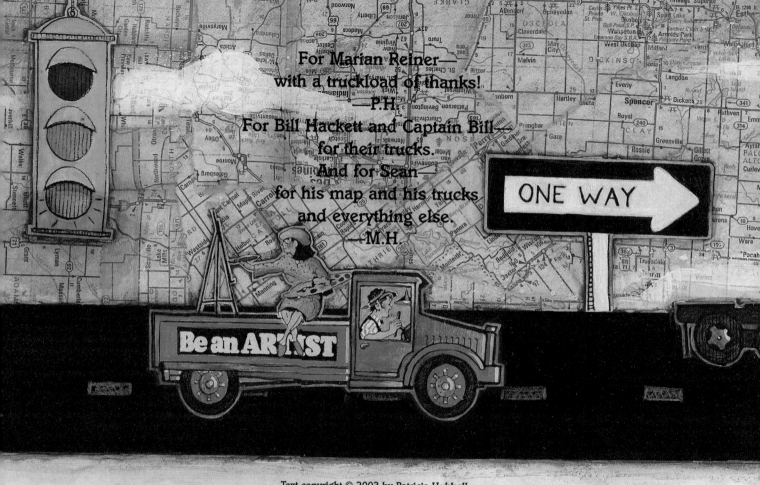

For Marian Reiner—
with a truckload of thanks!
—P.H.
For Bill Hackett and Captain Bill—
for their trucks.
And for Sean—
for his map and his trucks
and everything else.
—M.H.

ONE WAY

Be an ARTIST

Amazon Publishing, Attn: Amazon Children's Publishing, P.O. Box 400818, Las Vegas, NV 89140
www.amazon.com/amazonchildrenspublishing

Library of Congress Cataloging-in-Publication Data
Hubbell, Patricia.
Trucks: whizz! zoom! rumble! / by Patricia Hubbell ; illustrations by Megan Halsey.
p. cm.
Summary: A rhyming look at many different kinds of trucks, from eighteen-wheelers to ice cream trucks, as they go about their business.
ISBN-13: 978-0-7614-5328-4 (paperback)
ISBN-10: 0-7614-5328-8 (paperback)
ISBN-10: 0-7614-5124-2 (hardcover)
[1. Trucks—Fiction. 2. Stories in rhyme.] I. Halsey, Megan, ill. II. Title.
PZ8.3.H848 Wh 2003 [E]—dc21 2002008320

The text of this book is set in 24 point Italia medium.
The illustrations were rendered in collage.
Original hardcover book design by Adam Mietlowski

Printed in China
3 5 6 4

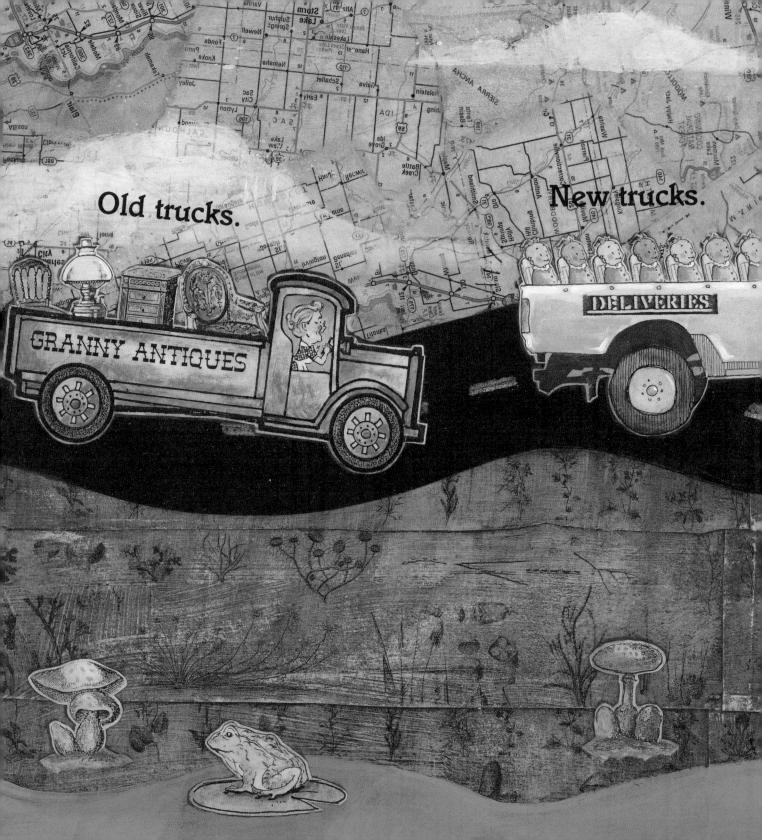

Old trucks.

New trucks.

Going-to-the-zoo trucks.

Red trucks.

Blue trucks.

Bringing-toys-to-you trucks.

Trailer trucks with lots of wheels.

Trucks that carry automobiles.

Trucks at rest stops getting gas,
whose drivers wave each time you pass.

Heavy trucks.

Light trucks. Whizzing-through-the-night trucks.

Garbage trucks.

Tow trucks.

Pack Mule Towing

Plowing-up-the-snow trucks

Arctic Plow Co.

Trucks that **RUMBLE**,

ROAR,

and

shriek.

Trucks that **putter**,

Canary Construction

Granny Antiques

Ghost Hill Farm

groan,

and *creak.*

Trucks, trucks, trucks on the long, long road.

Ice-cream trucks.

Fire trucks.

Carpenters-for-hire trucks.

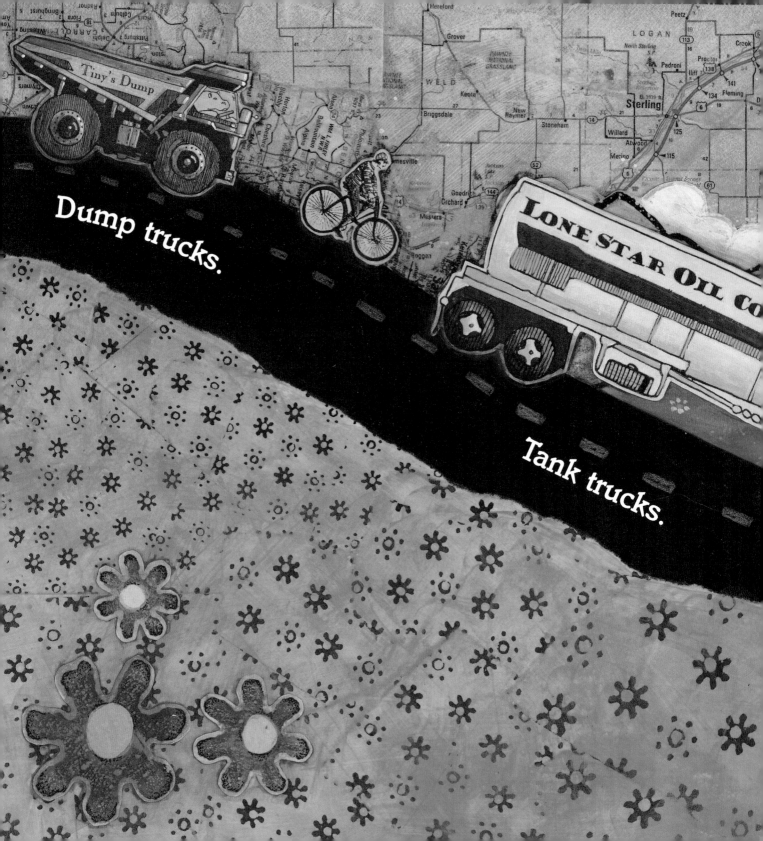

Dump trucks.

Tank trucks.

Going-to-the-bank trucks.

Trucks with horses. Trucks with hens.

Trucks with big pink pigs in pens.

Trucks that *rush*

and *whizz*

and **zoom**.

Bakery

Be an ARTIST

FRESH SANDWICHES

Trucks that **bang**

Shepherd & Sons
Waste Management

and **HONK**

Addyville Company #4

and

boom.

Tiny's Dump

Tandem trucks
that go by twos.
Trucks that bring us
all the news.

Moving vans.
Concrete mixers.
Ambulances.
Flat-tire fixers.

Auntie Sue's and Tommy's trucks.

Here you go in YOUR truck!

Zoom,
zoom,
zoom,
down the
long,
long
road.

Trucks go north, south, east, and west.

Then,

they

rest.

NIGHT

STOP

MOTEL

COLOR TV CABLE
DIRECT DIAL PHONES
CRIBS · KITCHENETTE

VACANCY

Sleepwell Mattress
Company

Made in the USA
Charleston, SC
27 November 2013